THE
STATIC
HERD

BETH STEIDLE

Published by Calamari Press, NY, NY
www.clamaripress.com

First Edition

ISBN 978-1-940853-03-1

for W.E.S.

1947-2013

Witnessed over time, a change in sound and appearance:

Deer: from Old English *deor* "animal, beast, any sort of wild creature." From Proto-Germanic *deuzam*, "animal" (as opposed to man), and *dheusom,* "creature that breathes." Related to Lithuanian *dusti* (to gasp, to sigh), Lithuanian *dvesti* (to exhale, to perish), Russian *dusa* (breath, spirit), Russian *dvochat* (to cough), Sanskrit *dhvaṁsati* (he falls to dust).

He was wild when they found him. Crawling like a wounded deer on buckled fours in the middle of the road. A clot of tumor lodged in an airway. There was blood and vomit on his face and chest.

The man who drove him to the emergency room would later renovate the kitchen.

Meanwhile, his son was on the way to the same hospital to receive the first round of rabies shots. In broad daylight, a raccoon had attacked the dogs in pursuit of their water bowl. The son had beaten the red-eyed, frothing thing off with a stick.

Afterword, the son stood in the kitchen with blood on his face and could not confidently say that it had not gotten into his eyes.

There was confusion at the hospital because the father and the son have the same name. When the son arrived just minutes after the father, the nurse kept tapping the privacy screen over her computer screen and repeating, *but you're already here.*

From where the mother sat the computer screen appeared as a flat, milky plane.

Later, after the kitchen was renovated, she painted a forest around the border, just below the stark place where the wall meets the ceiling. Spattered boughs were splayed over the doorways and windows. The father said, *you've ruined it.* She said, *but you said you wanted to die out in the open.*

The solution is to turn the whole world inside out.

I

This examination was performed on 08/19/2011 at 11:34 AM.

Patient Name: S, W
Admission Date: 08/19/11
DOB: 05/12/1947
Age: 64
Sex: M
Pt status: ADM IN
Admitting physician: THOMR
Visit: H00957677
MR: L791032
JOB#: 13397824/478333677
Report: Today I learned the year of my
father's birth.

FINDINGS: There is a large high attenuation mass in the left frontal lobe. There is considerable surrounding this mass. There is 6 mm shift to the right. There is effacement noted on the left. There is a. There is. There is. There is no. This is unchanged when compared to the previous examination performed earlier on the same day. This critical finding was discussed with Dr. J at 2 AM by the on-call radiologist Dr. Q.

HISTORY: An immaculate birth. The silhouette emerged radiant and immediately leaned towards the sun. Favor a heartbreaker. Favor a hellraiser.

IMPRESSION: Venation of the underbelly reveals splintered boughs. The forest opens when prodded. The body's fields are clear. The angles are sharp. The bones are soft. The orbits cave in to the eyes. The eyes are faded plums, damp and quiet. The mother does not believe the baby should be touched too often or too long. Some water moves over and shadows over that.

Patient Name: S, W
Admission Date: 08/19/11
DOB: 05/12/1947
Age: 64
Sex: M
MR#: L791045
Visit#: H009576771
Patient Location: L4N L413-01
Report#: 0819-01460
Order Number(s): 1-0819-00037
Exam: CT BRAIN W and W/O CONTRAST
Report: That as the body reduces finitely, the numbers increase exponentially. She said something about windows.

HISTORY: 1. In 1969 his mother rose in the night to go to the bathroom. Midway, a vessel in her brain burst. She died instantly. 2. What remains of her is an ambrotype hung in the window. Beside a glass negative of Horseshoe Falls. 3. We are in perpetual descent. Dark, inverted coils tumble over the ledge. 4. On occasion light passes through her profile. She is lit. 5. How the body looks when closed. How the body looks when open. Light touching where it should never. 6. They say I resemble her the most, but if so he gives no indication. This river, her ghost through my skin.

FINDINGS: There is partial effacement of the sylvian fissure on the left at the level of the basal cisterns. There is mass effect. The appearance is concerning. The sylvian fissure cleaves the world in two. Memories of birth swirl at the base of the trench. There is black water. The appearance is concerning for hemorrhage. There is occasional, sublime flicker. Yes. Stuffed to the gills with longing. A sudden streak of light minnows until it encounters. There is a heterogeneously high attenuation mass 4.2 x 4.9 x 4.5. Through that which it cannot pass. Until today I did not know the year of my father's birth. The appearance is concerning for hemorrhage, including hemorrhage within a brain mass. Everything is sunken, yet capable of being remembered. By the time it bobs to the surface it has changed utterly, lost its shape and secret radiance. So let's, up, and pronto. Now is the time to undress. To bathe and/or swim.

Patient Name: S, W
Admission Date: 08/19/11
DOB: 05/12/1947
Age: 64
Sex: M
MR#: L7910400
Visit#: H009576761
DICTATE DATE: 08/19/11 0752
TRANS DATE: 08/19/11 0754
Patient Location: LICU L.01-01
Report#: 0820-0020
Order Number(s): 1-0819-0089
Exam: CT BRAIN W/O CONTRAST
Report: That by transubstantiation the wolf becomes the deer. The following acts are pure in intention.

HISTORY: 1. His grandfather died in the corner of our living room. On Thanksgiving my father said, *I don't know what happened to that chair.* 2. On Thanksgiving my mother said, *the doctor says that once the cancer gets into the lungs, you suffocate on yourself.* 3. He believes that death is finite. She believes in heaven and hell. She believes in limbo. 4. She believes she saw his grandfather's ghost hovering at the end of the hallway. Wire-rimmed glasses and oiled hair, a slick side part, and a belly slit with a gold watch chain. 5. The hallway runs between the bedrooms where we slept as children. 6. He gives no indication. Ghosts, rivers, etc. Footsteps heard in parts of the house where people are not.

IMPRESSION: Examination degraded by motion artifact. Limited study due to motion artifact. There is a murmur in the undergrowth. I agree. This is in agreement with. Yes. There has been a significant shift.

Patient Name: S, W
Admission Date: 08/19/11
DOB: 05/12/1947
Age: 64
Sex: M
MR#: M4884530
Visit#: V00898648
DICTATE DATE: 08/19/11 0956
TRANS DATE: 08/19/11 1456
Patient Location: ER
Report#: 0820-0208
Order Number(s): 1-0819-0016
Exam: CHEST SINGLE VIEW
Report: Further, that if an animal is a machine, and a music box is a machine, then according to the transitive property an animal is a music box.

HISTORY: 1. The yellow dog was flung out of a car in the middle of the night. Where I come from we say *the thing was dropped*. 2. My father named the dog after his grandfather, the ghost. 3. For nine years, the dog left the bodies of small mammals and portions of larger ones on the front steps. For nine years, deer legs piled up on the lawn. Formed a static herd, bore up the invisible husks of upper halves. 4. Our bellies are full of pine needles and air. The heart is only a cave with four chambers where jealous eels nest. 5. What is held inside the mouth. What returns between the teeth. If and so, according to the transitive property.

TECHNIQUE: They've gone inside now.

FINDINGS: Darkly studded inlet, brimming cisterns. Of blood and other things. Evaluation of the right hemithorax reveals the body gone ecstatic with growth. The heart enlarged in size. The liver enlarged in size. The right node of the thyroid absent. The spine divulging its final arc, a rare, slow curl like a nocturnal fern.

IMPRESSIONS: O ecstatic heart! A deer midbirth will run nonetheless. An animal when threatened will attempt to make itself appear larger. Everything is known. Witness hipbones slough dust and scales. Cross-sections of torso aligned, backlit. The appearance is concerning. The finding critical. I remember the exact silhouette of her form when she sunk into the Colorado and began to swim. The river turned an oxblood where she rustled up the silt. I loved her exactly. I don't know you at all. There are rivers inside of you. That much we know.

IMPRESSIONS: At birth, the chest can be flattened between two hands. It's true history repeats itself. The circuitry gone sour. There's a nick in the loop. There's a murmur in the undergrowth. The hematoma was the size of an average lemon. Everyone comprehends this size. The size recalls the hands. Hence the overuse of fruit as a metaphor. The texture, color of an eggplant. The lungs too are turning pears. The brain, the bones. The body left to bear its dark crop, a finite ripening. Here: fingers enter the mouth. Now: leave it again. Something related to breathing. I used to speak more freely. I used to speak more freely.

II

OPERATIVE REPORT:

JOB#: 1397824/476443107

1. LEFT FRONTAL CRANIOTOMY FOR EVACUTATION OF INTRAPARENCHYMAL HEMATOMA
2. RESECTION OF LEFT FRONTAL LOBE LESION

PREOPERATIVE DIAGNOSIS:
Left frontal intraparenchymal hematoma.

POSTOPERATIVE DIAGNOSES:
1. Left frontal intraparenchymal hematoma.
2. Suspected renal cell carcinoma, metastasis.

INDICATIONS FOR PROCEDURE: Briefly, this patient presented with headaches. A metastatic lesion is suspected. The patient was presented with the options. The family was presented with the options. Everyone subsumed to what was recommended.

OPERATIVE NOTE: Patient brought to the operating theater. Patient doubles helter skelter. Fingers in the mouth, leave it again. Patient goes down as expected. A time-out performed per protocol. Patient arranged in a supine pose. Patient's head pinned with a Mayfield 3. Preparatory skin marks ticked crown to helix. Hair removed with surgical clippers. Cleansing of the face. The neck rotated slightly to the right. The neck brought into a bit of an extension. Whereupon the view improves. Becomes panoramic. We pull into the scenic overlook. Our faces have been in our hands our whole lives. She says, *everyone out of the car this instant.* What begins in the valley. Ruptured fruit from here to horizon.

OPERATIVE NOTE: Blush of iodine, followed by draping. Confirm the presence of all necessary imaging tools. With these modern eyes these modern visions, ersatz saints. These days nothing escapes us. Cameras enter easily.

ELSEWHERE: In the barren wasteland of our waiting, commercials achieve a circadian rhythm. What happens in Vegas stays in Vegas. Blind taste tests reveal the generic is a dynamo. Bathroom tiles bleach to white under the influence of mystic bubbles. There is no mildew. There is computer generated starlight. I am so close to becoming a believer. My mother says, *did you know that all of the angels can fit on the head of a pin?* My brother says, *it's true a grown man can swim through the artery of a blue whale without grazing its walls.*

OPERATIVE NOTE: Along the surface, an abnormal encounter. Fervent Mars, we searched so long for water. We scoured for bacteria in the vestigial ice. We wanted more and more. We sent our greetings out in every language. With our many tongues we identified ourselves as children. We asked the darkness if it had eaten. We said to the darkness, goodnight ladies and gentlemen. Now we know to keep one ear to the sky, and one to the earth in the event that you surprise us from within.

1.1 cm x .8 cm

1.1 cm x 1.3 cm

8 mm x 9 mm

5 cm

1.5 cm x 1.2 cm

5 mm

6 mm

3 cm x 2.2 cm

4.8 cm x 5.3 cm

1.5 cm x 1.2 cm

2.1 cm x 2.3 cm

4.1 cm x 4 cm

1 cm x 1.3 cm

4.2 cm x 4.9 cm x 4.5 cm

7 mm

9 mm

4 mm

3.8 cm x 3.8 cm

PROCEDURE IN DETAIL: A portion of the face folded in on itself. Reference: the peeling firmament. Wherein bone is the lampflood. This was never debatable. What we want swims behind the light, fiddling with the switches. A closed loop of faith. At a depth of about 6 mm a substantial is encountered. Portions of this are liquified and portions are clotted. This is evacuated. Evacuate all meaning. What's coming. They say you can't predict a black horse. A gloved hand. An outbreak of cyclones, each equipped with a singular dazzling eye, a mouth like a vacuum. A clot of weeping women, insect below the neck. A cicadian lament most often translated, *lawnmower lawnmower.*

OPERATIVE NOTE: Administration of anticonvulsants and steroids. Dulling agent injected along the line of incision. An area of abnormal tissue encountered. Frozen sections are inconclusive, but suspicious. Like a field, he is irrigated copiously. Hemostasis once again assured. Yes, yes. For decades enter and return have been synonymous. He enters, he returns. Bloody sentinels at attention along the ridge line.

ELSEWHERE: We are surrounded by soft chairs. We think of the bones of infants. Decadent and vibrant, death knells fan across the tables: *Goodhousekeeping, Time, Newsweek, Better Homes & Gardens.* The waiting room is garnished with yawning orchids, their dumb and violet jaws. She says, *based on the plant life this must be a good hospital.* The social worker moves from one family to another. We wait. We witness dozens of 15-minute meals. There are no missteps. Everything looks incredibly easy 100% of the time. Every chef has the whitest teeth. I say, *all the devils too.*

FINDINGS: Elsewhere, there is mass effect. There is shift to the right. Elsewhere there is no hemorrhage. There is no other mass or shift. Elsewhere.

OPERATIVE NOTE: The dura is opened in a cruciate fashion. Inspected down to the level of. Three membranes envelope the brain: the dura mater, arachnoid mater, pia mater. From medieval Latin: hard mother, spider mother, soft mother. As in, the knife passes through a trio of women. Her ghost in my skin. In the shape of an X. In 1969 he lost her. Yes, I am afraid. I am ashamed. These days I find my hand on my belly more often than not. He says, *the secret to a long life is to never get married.* Her hands are green from the painted boughs. She crawls across the kitchen floor and weeps. At a depth of about 6 mm, a substantial is encountered. The dog named after his grandfather was buried inside a black garbage bag behind the barn. He is sealed with intermittent sutures. Three plates used to reaffix the skull.

OPERATIVE NOTE: Images enter the eye upside down and are righted. Corneas designated for harvest. She said something about windows. At breakfast, he asks to be burned, then fed to the earth. A drain brought out through a separate stab incision. Skin closed with staples. Et voila, et voila. We stop counting at fifty. The forehead anointed. The hair irrevocably separated. The feet dried with the hair. The face dried with the hair. She imagines Mary Magdalene in the damp cave beside the shoreline, the damp cave of the heart, the martyr's palm tickling her breast. Yes, with seven devils and the lemon cast out.

OPERATIVE NOTE: What follows is a standard dressing. The drapes removed. The patient taken out from the headrest, placed back in neutral position. He is rolled on his side like an infant. In preparation for emergence.

CONDITION: Stable, extubated, neurologically intact.

COUNTS: All needle, sponge, and cottonoid counts are reported correct at the end of the operation.

ESTIMATED BLOOD LOSS: 150 mL

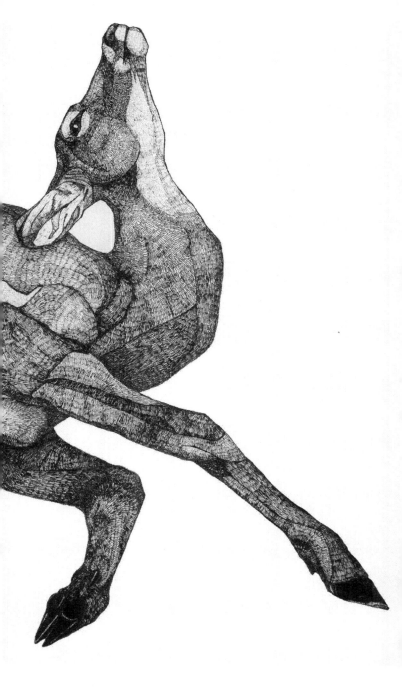

III

2 cm x 1.5 cm x 0.7 cm

FINDINGS: Specimen is received fresh. Specimen consists of several fragments of pink-tan to brown soft-blood clot measuring 2 x 1.5 x 0.7. Favor metastatic RCC. Favor heliotropic. Favor fields, open space. Favor 6 to 12 months of diminishing. The coyotes' ghost-wails roll in all night. All the calendars feature wolves and foxes. She rolls over and murmurs, *for god's sake just stop.* Organs shift to accommodate what's been taken: post-nephrectomy, post-craniotomy. There's nothing to be done about the lungs. We favor dogs. Favor herons. Favor decoys of ducks, bellies filed to a flat plane. We swim very quietly. Something passes overhead. We wait. For frozen study.

IMPRESSION: There is a tube that drains blood from the crown. The red thread crosses his forehead and goes off in the distance. Like children we become distracted before we reach the conclusion. Often we find the finish line by sweet mistake. There is saline pumped in through the elbow crook. There is a bag of urine tied to the bedleg. This is filling while that is emptying. O pastoral! The phrase you seek is: *what a fabulous tour.*

IMPRESSIONS: 1. He circles the ICU in a blue gown. In fact, there is a swarm of gowned forms. Revenants mucking up the air quality. 2. The housecoats are patterned with vibrant blooms. There are transitory gardens observed making loops. When a species goes unhunted. His shadow passes ten times over. 3. He says they said to perform ten rounds daily. He says they said, *we all want more than what we have.* He says they said, *yes but from what I hear you are a very lucky man.*

IMPRESSION: Times passes. Dinner is served. When he ordered, the menu was very clear. There were three hollow boxes. Clip art of banners and starbursts. The Salisbury steak was specified "homemade." Yet when it arrives on the plastic tray, its uniform thickness and pristine circumference suggest otherwise. We rally: it's possible with rolling pins! A cookie cutter! O pristine circumference. We flail our arms to compensate for his diluted gestures. The bandage coiled about the crown. Reference: cartoon lunatic. Jelly in the sockets and a puppet's jaw. Over the years our beliefs have withered on the vine. Our mother is the sole survivor. We leave her trembling in the chapel. Where light filters through the glass belly of a saint. She sways on her knees like a nervous parakeet. Light comes through the shepherd, then through the lamb. Her glasses are huge, her lips drawn to a tiny slit. With her hands she pushes down the air. She chirps, *but but but.*

FINDINGS: There is a child in the bed over there. His room is puffed up with mylar balloons, dreamily resisting their ribbons. An animal when threatened will attempt to make itself appear larger. There are clusters of bells sounding faintly. Elsewhere. His swaddled head sways like a dazed turtle, the dumb jaw hangs open. The spoon misses the mouth. Corn dribbles down the neck and falls inside the gown. What follows is sublimation. With wild arms and giant mouths. With giant mouths filled with giant nights, we ask if he would like to be fed.

IMPRESSION: Statistics predict 6 to 12 months of diminishing half-lives. Leaning towards death like a blown tulip. Sitting on the kitchen steps in the huge light, he heaves up a single shrimp. Melanic stippling in the eyemoons and along the temples. *Whatever it is,* he says, *I'm sure it's not good.*

COURSE: Anticoagulants taken faithfully in the AM. Followed by small molecules. This will prolong survival by 1 to 2 months. He shaves his head preemptively. His long, thick hair had been his pride his whole life. Which when thrown in the garden is known to keep the deer from eating. Elsewhere the white curtain flounders like a ghost. We are unarmed. I gather all the dead and hang them on my father's shrinking frame. Like gowns, a palimpsest of quivering forms. The modern death is a process of extension, bred like the long bellies of useless dogs. Of great lengths and infinite strings. Repeat: we are unarmed. He declines the removal of birthmarks. We strike refresh. Decoys float on the dresser. Refresh. The bone flap elevated and stored on the back table.

IMPRESSION: The body made when released into air. It's gone and then some. The after-image itches in the wing. Sitting in the pickup, he notes the treatment in the calendar. The forehead exhibits burn marks. The month is fox chasing rabbit through landscape. Shed antlers have been observed on the dashboard. Saplings have been observed on the floor. The term is unremarkable.

COURSE: He goes down of his own accord. The nurse pins his head. All measures which can be carried out without touching must be taken. She clips the mask over his face. The mask is a vivid yellow grate. The mask has been specially molded for the contours of his eyes and nose. Measurements were precisely taken. The mask honeycombs over his bald head. It is very important that the mask fit snugly. Between treatments this hollow version of his face is stowed in a closet. On a shelf of frozen veils.

IMPRESSION: The brumal season creeps in without notice. Like every other winter inches itself along by its teeth. The problem is what happens within. My eyes are closed and will never open. Within cells double and double. Last legs shy beneath the dinner table.

MEANWHILE: She winds the clocks obsessively. The idea is to get every room to chime in sync.

IMPRESSION: I used to be less afraid. I used to speak more freely. Back when the blood was an open river. Before the horses of the apocalypse began to swim, muzzles snorting through the current. A froth is churning in the heart chambers. I know because I can hear it. He looks so tiny in the easy chair. Bridles spin dark arterial loops.

IMPRESSION: Mongrel dogs wild at the chain. One with a pale eye, dark eye. They say that one's hexed. Something went down where the dairy farmer throws the stillborn calves. There, behind the stonewall fence. We found hoofprints which were unidentifiable. He crawled on his hands and knees to find the neighbor had gone on vacation and then began inching out into the road. The dissection was carried out in August, twelve days after my 30th birthday. Things were done with a #10 scalpel and later an 11. Anatomical references used once again. This means the surgeons looked at pictures with him wide open. The field guide is a notoriously useless catalog of images which cannot be matched to their living counterparts. *Try to count the number of legs,* she said. Cut with a current. Use the palm-span to estimate the wing-print. The trill of the thrush sounds digital and evokes a modem. *Ee-oh-lay* in the undergrowth. Something done with an elevator and two bur holes. The intended. This procedure was standard. Mottled eyes deceive on the wing. It's just that everything moves away so quickly.

IMPRESSION: Now when we sleep you are inside of us. Our dreams play out inside your chest, which is inside of us. Which from inside resembles a series of abstract folds. Now you are becoming light as it minnows into darkness. Now you are becoming darkness softly punctured with light. This particular firmament, this particular alignment of tumor and organ will not repeat.

COURSE: Go outside, stay up late. The pole star has dipped down, away. Spread blankets on the lawn, wait. Lay down with the hexed dog. Wait and wait. We wait for something marvelous. The rare comet, dragging its debris. The velvet peel of antlers like phosphorescent coils. In this light. We wait. This process of becoming interior. Everything is known. Nothing can be done.

Witnessed over time, a change in sound and appearance:

Effacement: 1. An obliteration of the features (as in he begs not to be seen) 2. An erasure (oneself) (he begs not to be seen) 3. A shy withdrawal (oneself) (he begs) 4. The thinning of the mother's walls (she begs) 5. The final state of pregnancy; from the onset of contractions to the birth of a child (she begs) (he begs not to be seen) See also: childbed, confinement, lying-in, parturiency, travail, labour, labor, birth, cervix, dilation, station, flaring funnel, bathing, swimming, field, deathbed, future joy (she begs), future grief (he begs) (I beg not to be seen)

IMPRESSION: In the fire hall, my father introduces himself at every table. The guests say, *my god, you're unrecognizable.* A bald Samson, a wasting Goliath. Today, we feast. Tomorrow we belly up with regret. Tomorrow I intend to refuse all things. It's been proven: the universe is hurtling outward. My brother's wife puts her hand on her stomach and keens. She is losing the baby. I am sitting so close. I suspect but do nothing. You know it's nothing more than a tadpole at this stage. My love is drowsy when I give it at all. I watch the tablecloth. I wait for cake. I lie down with the hexed dog. It was a birthday party, for god's sake.

COURSE: With a canine premonition shuffle off into the fields. Lie among the fallen trees, ruffled and sprung with mushrooms. Turkey Tail and Indian Pipe. Simply go off there. The body slowly opening, the body slowly settling down. The coyotes stumbling upon the gold mine inside the torso. Few people donate their corneas.

TECHNIQUE: Conjure the lush mongrel of future grief. Send it out to stalk the infinite strings. If you think you're better than this, you're not.

COURSE: Theretofore and hereafter, open upon waking. Practice weeping. The phone will go wild with brief and bioluminescent cycles. Practice restrained wails, soft gestures. Rewrite the little speech. Measure the weight of your grief, consider the skin. Evaluate the bones. Wait, wait. Cradle what appears at the feet. These are gifts from the feral mouth.

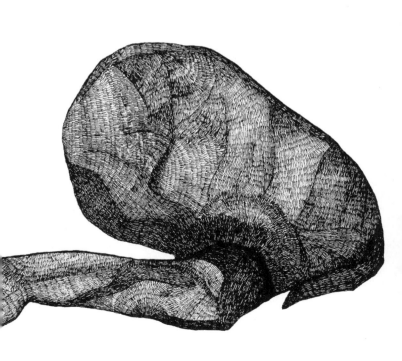

SPECIAL THANKS TO:

Derek White, Chuck Kinder, Ben Lerner, Peter Mishler, Aubrie Marrin, Ryan Murphy, Jeremy Patlen, Josephine Kovash, Adam Farkas, and Steve Colca.